For Uncle Jim and Aunt Aki Yamazaki, with love.
Thank you for keeping our family stories alive.

Text and illustrations copyright © 2013 by Katie Yamasaki
All Rights Reserved
HOLIDAY HOUSE is registered in the U.S. Patent and Trademark Office.
Printed and Bound in October 2012 at Toppan Leefung, DongGuan City, China.
The text typeface is Hiroshige.
The artwork was created with acrylic paint on canvas paper.
www.holidayhouse.com
First Edition
1 3 5 7 9 10 8 6 4 2

Library of Congress Cataloging-in-Publication Data
Yamasaki, Katie.
Fish for Jimmy: based on one family's experience in a Japanese American internment camp / Katie Yamasaki. — 1st ed.
p. cm.
Summary: When brothers Taro and Jimmy and their mother are forced to move from their home in California
to a Japanese internment camp in the wake of the 1941 Pearl Harbor bombing, Taro daringly escapes the camp
to find fresh fish for his grieving brother.
ISBN 978-0-8234-2375-0 (hardcover)
1. Japanese Americans—Evacuation and relocation, 1942-1945—Juvenile fiction.
[1. Japanese Americans—Evacuation and relocation, 1942-1945—Fiction. 2. Brothers—Fiction.]
I. Title.
PZ7.Y19157Fi 2013
[E]—dc23
2012006584

FISH FOR JIMMY

Inspired by One Family's Experience
in a Japanese American Internment Camp

Katie Yamasaki

Holiday House / New York

When Taro and Jimmy went to the ocean, Taro would tell Jimmy about the fish. The fish had taught Taro how to swim, he said. Jimmy hoped that one day he would be as strong and smart as Taro, that he too would learn the ways of the fish and the water.

Then Taro would point across the great Pacific Ocean and tell his brother stories about Japan, the land Mother and Father had left long ago in search of a better life.

The life they found in California was good indeed. Father and two other men opened a vegetable market. Farmers brought their vegetables to Father's market, and he would sell them to owners of small vegetable stands.

Some days, Mother helped by keeping track of the stock and greeting the vegetable stand owners as they searched for the ripest tomatoes and the leafiest lettuce.

But one night early in December 1941, Mother and Father frowned deeply
at what they heard on the radio. Japan had bombed Pearl Harbor, in Hawaii.
Taro and Jimmy wondered why their parents were so worried. Hawaii was
far away, and Japan even farther.

Bang! Bang! Bang! Mother answered the door to three men whose badges read FBI. The men told Father that, because he was Japanese, he posed a threat to America. Father tried to explain that he loved living in America. He had a home and a vegetable market and a family here. But the men said he had to go with them.

As Father left, he said to Taro,
"You are the man of the house now.
You must help your mother and take care of
Jimmy until I return." But Father would not return soon.
    One day signs went up all across California with orders
for people of Japanese descent.

Japan and America were at war, and Japanese people were forced to leave their homes and schools and jobs. Taking only what they could carry, they boarded crowded buses with covered windows.

The buses carried Mother, Jimmy, Taro, and others to a desolate land where they were forced to live in tiny barracks surrounded by guarded fences.

In the dusty internment camp, Jimmy lost his appetite.
"Whose child is that?" the cooks whispered, glancing
at Jimmy. "He hasn't eaten since we've been here."
Mother bowed her head in shame and desperation.

Author's Note

While this story is dressed up a little for dramatic effect, it is based on a true event that occurred in July 1927. Throughout the first half of the 1900s, a group calling themselves the Ku Klux Klan terrorized Southern blacks and the whites who sympathized with them. Covered in white sheets, they often did their work at night (hence, the nickname Night Riders), setting fire to homes and lynching men accused of false crimes. Most decent folks couldn't even think about the Klan without shivering in their shoes.

At the time the story takes place, Bessie Smith traveled with her revue, The Harlem Frolics, in a custom-made train car that took them all over the South. This made life a lot easier for Bessie, since there were few hotels that would accept black performers. They could carry their own tent—the longest pole just fit down the center aisle—instruments, and vending equipment, as well as sleep, eat, and relax there. The car had seven state rooms, a kitchen and bathroom with hot and cold running water, and bunks below that slept up to thirty-five people.

On that July evening, the performers had set up for the night near the city of Concord, North Carolina. The electric generator they used to light up the stage was creating additional heat that, together with the stifling temperatures of the July evening, made some of the performers sick. One of the musicians knew he was close to passing out, so he stepped outside to get some air. There, around a corner of the tent, he saw half a dozen Klansmen pulling up the tent stakes. What they intended to do

exactly, nobody knows, but they were certainly trying to collapse the tent. Luckily, the Klansmen did not see him and he ran back to the stage and told Bessie, who had just finished a set.

As the audience hollered for her to return and sing some more, Bessie ordered the prop boys to follow and found the Klansmen. As soon as the prop boys saw the hooded men, they ran off, but Bessie ran toward the Klan, pulled herself up to her full six feet in height, and demanded to know just what they thought they were doing.

According to eyewitness reports, Bessie cursed and shouted for quite some time, ending with: "You just pick up them sheets and run." After a moment of astonished silence, the hooded figures turned around and disappeared into the darkness. Bessie finished off by finding the prop boys and telling them: "You ain't nothin' but a bunch of sissies."

Then she went back into the tent and mounted the stage as if history had not just been made on that hot July evening. Her selfless act of heroism may have saved hundreds of innocent lives that night.

If you are interested in learning more about the life and times of Bessie Smith, here are two biographies that have been written about her.

Bessie Smith by Elaine Feinstein, Viking, 1985.
Somebody's Angel Child by Carman Moore, T. Y. Crowell, 1969.

To my dear friend Terri McElwee, who helps
girls and women find their strength.
—S.S.

To all the young aspiring artists—
always follow your passion and
strive to paint a beautiful world.
—J.H.

G. P. PUTNAM'S SONS

A division of Penguin Young Readers Group

Published by The Penguin Group

Penguin Group (USA) Inc., 375 Hudson Street, New York, NY 10014, U.S.A.

Penguin Group (Canada), 90 Eglinton Avenue East, Suite 700, Toronto, Ontario, Canada M4P 2Y3 (a division of Pearson Penguin Canada Inc.).

Penguin Books Ltd, 80 Strand, London WC2R 0RL, England.

Penguin Ireland, 25 St. Stephen's Green, Dublin 2, Ireland (a division of Penguin Books Ltd.).

Penguin Group (Australia), 250 Camberwell Road, Camberwell, Victoria 3124, Australia (a division of Pearson Australia Group Pty Ltd).

Penguin Books India Pvt Ltd, 11 Community Centre, Panchsheel Park, New Delhi - 110 017, India.

Penguin Group (NZ), Cnr Airborne and Rosedale Roads, Albany, Auckland 1310, New Zealand (a division of Pearson New Zealand Ltd).

Penguin Books (South Africa) (Pty) Ltd, 24 Sturdee Avenue, Rosebank, Johannesburg 2196, South Africa.

Penguin Books Ltd, Registered Offices: 80 Strand, London WC2R 0RL, England.

Library of Congress Cataloging-in-Publication Data   Stauffacher, Sue, 1961– Bessie Smith and the night riders /
by Sue Stauffacher ; illustrated by John Holyfield.   p. cm.   Summary: Black blues singer Bessie Smith
single-handedly scares off Ku Klux Klan members who are trying to disrupt her show one hot July night
in Concord, North Carolina. Includes historical note. Includes bibliographical references (p. 31).
1. Smith, Bessie, 1894–1937—Juvenile fiction. [1. Smith, Bessie, 1894–1937—Fiction.
2. Blues (Music)—Fiction. 3. Ku Klux Klan (1915–)—Fiction. 4. African Americans—Fiction.
5. North Carolina—Fiction.] I. Holyfield, John, ill. II. Title.   PZ7.S8055Bes 2006
[E]—dc22   2005010399   ISBN 0-399-24237-6
10 9 8 7 6 5 4 3 2 1   First Impression

Photo credit page 30: Music Division, the New York Public Library for the Performing Arts, Astor, Lenox and Tilden Foundations.